ghost writer™

THE JUNGLE BOOK

© 2019 Sesame Workshop. Ghostwriter, and associated characters, trademarks, and design elements are owned and licensed by Sesame Workshop. All rights reserved.

Published by Sourcebooks Wonderland, an Imprint of Sourcebooks Kids.
Sourcebooks and the colophon are registered trademarks of Sourcebooks.
All Rights Reserved.
P.O. Box 4410, Naperville, Illinois 60567-4410
(630) 961-3900
Fax: (630) 961-2168
sourcebooks.com

sesameworkshop.org

Design by Whitney Manger
Craft illustrations by Jenny Bee

Library of Congress data is on file with the publisher.

Printed and bound in the United States of America.
MA 10 9 8 7 6 5 4 3 2 1

ghost writer™

THE JUNGLE BOOK

by Rudyward Kipling

adapted by Karuna Riazi

illustrated by Oriol Vidal

with an introduction by Kwame Alexander

sourcebooks
wonderland

SESAME WORKSHOP®

Dear Rock Star Reader,

Books are like amusement parks, and this one here is a roller coaster. As you begin your reading adventure, I just want to chime in and say get ready for an incredibly amazing experience reimagining some of your favorite books. That's right: between the pages of this book, Ghostwriter is bringing your favorite characters to life to help solve a mystery. How cool is that?

I bet you think that because I'm an author, I love to read. Well, you're right! In order to become a good writer, you gotta be a great reader. Every time you read a meaningful or magical poem or story or really clever post, you're instantly transformed and sometimes transported to new ideas and worlds: sports arenas, foreign lands, outer space, other times in history, and even other kids' lives. But I wasn't always that way.

When I was twelve, I thought reading was uncool. Why? Because my dad chose huge, boring books he thought

I should read. After a few years of that torture, my mom encouraged me to pick out my own books at our local library, and I found my way back to finding reading cool. (I guess you could say I started choosing my own rides at the amusement park.) Then I started reading everything—chapter books, short stories, comic books, biographies, and, of course, poetry. Ghostwriter, like my mom, believes that there's a perfect book for every kid out there. And the one you're reading could be yours.

I love getting lost in a good story, and there are so, so many great stories out there just waiting for you. Our friend Ghostwriter is gonna help you find them—and then rock your world one page at a time.

I thank you for your attention, and I'm outta here!

Kwame Alexander

Poet, Educator, and Newbery Medal–winning author of *The Crossover*

chapter 1

There's a lot to love about the Indian jungle. Especially if you're a wolf.

Mowgli learned that early on. The Seeonee Wolf Pack, his family, lived in dens on the bank of a beautiful river. Every day, he woke to its cheerful gurgling. He'd run out with the other wolf cubs. They tumbled through the sun-warmed water until another cub's mother dragged them out, her teeth carefully clamped on the back of their necks.

"Be careful with Mowgli," she'd warn.

But Mowgli didn't want to be careful. There were mangoes to shake out of the treetops. The ripe yellow ones oozed sweetness over his fingers. The small, sour green ones made him and his wolf brothers, Sharaad and Viaan, stick out their tongues and shake them until the sting went away. Little weasel-like mongooses came out of their burrows to wrestle with them, if the wolves asked nicely. Overhead, colorful birds called out greetings and reported the weather in the clouds. "It looks like rain in an hour! Be ready to run back home!" or "The sun is shining! Play on, little wolf cubs!"

Mowgli was happy. How could he not be when he was surrounded by his wolf family and living in the best jungle in the world?

Mowgli sat under his favorite banyan tree and watched his brothers coax the mongooses from their holes. He'd been playing, too, but the hot sun on his smooth skin had made him sleepy.

Besides, he wanted to think.

He was confused about his name. *Mowgli* meant "little frog," but Mowgli knew he was

definitely *not* a frog. He'd watched frogs hop from lily pad to lily pad on the river. His skin was firm, brown, and warm—not slimy or green, like theirs.

"I don't look like a little frog," Mowgli had told his parents. "Why did you name me that?"

"You're good at swimming," his father had said.

"You like to hop up into trees, and your brothers can't do that," his mother had said.

Mowgli wasn't furry like his wolf brothers and cousins. His tongue wasn't as long as theirs. He didn't have their sharp claws or beautiful, gleaming teeth. His parents treated him differently, too. His mother never let his brothers bite him when they were wrestling. He wasn't allowed to go into the middle of the river without someone's furry back to cling to with his long fingers. And what proper wolf had fingers?

Mowgli was very sure his parents weren't telling the whole truth about his name. It was all very strange. Why was he different from everyone else?

"How can I be a frog if I'm not slimy?" he said aloud to himself.

"A frog? You?" The silky voice curled around his shoulders moments before a velvety black tail settled there.

"Bagheera!" Mowgli whirled around. "Why do you always sneak up on me like that? What are you doing here?"

Bagheera the panther let out a great, big yawn. "Your father's returning from the hunt soon. I'm quite hungry. I was hoping for an invitation to family dinner."

Mowgli laughed and rubbed Bagheera's soft chin. "Of course you can come."

His wolf brothers were always cautious around

Bagheera. The panther was fast and strong and could knock you off your feet before you even noticed his paw move. But Mowgli thought of Bagheera as his fun uncle. Sure, the panther could be a know-it-all, but it was in a good way. Bagheera always looked out for him.

"Why are you sitting here, asking yourself silly questions?" said Bagheera. "How could you be a frog? Look at yourself. Not a patch of green or a wart to be found."

Mowgli stretched out his fingers and flexed them, a frown on his face. "I know. But what else could I be? I don't look like the other wolves."

"So you want to be a *frog*?" Bagheera arched his eyebrows.

"Of course I don't want to be a frog. I want to be part of the jungle," Mowgli said. "I want to belong here."

"And who says you don't?" Bagheera's tail

flicked away a pesky fly. "This is your jungle. You've lived here your whole life."

Mowgli closed his eyes and breathed in. The warm spice of the air filled his lungs—freshly turned earth, ripening bananas, and the distant musk of a passing jackal. This was his jungle. He knew it in his blood, just as he knew what every plant was, where to find the juiciest berries, and which rocks would skip best over the river's surface. But why did he still feel so confused?

Suddenly, a loud scuffle erupted in front of them. Mowgli and Bagheera both snapped their heads forward as Viaan and Sharaad tumbled over a pile of rocks.

Sharaad's claws scratched against stone and sparks flew into Viaan's face.

Viaan reared back. "Ow! Ow! What was that?" he howled.

Bagheera leaped toward them. "Are you all right, Viaan?"

Sharaad was already licking his brother's cheeks, examining the skin for bruises.

At the sight of the panther, both cubs jumped, but then Viaan nodded. "I'm okay," he said shakily. "That spark burned my cheek."

"I hate those sparks," Sharaad growled. "They gleam like fireflies but pierce your skin like hot thorns."

"Step on a flame flower, young cub, and then you will feel real pain," Bagheera said. "You'll be all right, Viaan. Let your brother lick your wound."

"A flame flower? What's that?" Mowgli asked.

"The flame flower stings worse than a spark and spreads as quickly as a bramblebush."

Mowgli leaned forward, spellbound.

A dangerous, beautiful flower? He thought he knew every plant in the jungle, but he'd never heard of this one before. Did this flower sear your tongue like a licked ember? Was its scent warm like ripe fruit? Questions tumbled through his mind.

"A flame flower is not something any of you would see, though," Bagheera said, examining one paw. "Only humans are foolish enough to grow them and keep them around."

Mowgli was confused. "Humans? What are humans?"

Before his brothers or the panther could answer, a low howl broke through the underbrush. The familiar sound warmed Mowgli's heart. His mother, Raksha, was calling them.

"Come on, Mowgli!" Viaan yelped excitedly. "Father must be home!"

Sharaad and Viaan hurried off, but Mowgli waited.

"What are humans, Bagheera? Are they a type of bear? Or bird? Or maybe a bee? And these flame flowers—why do they grow them?"

"If you were to go looking for the flame flower, not that I'm saying you should, I'd keep my eye to the ground and head west." Bagheera prowled into the bushes, pausing only to call over his shoulder, "If you find it, you might get some answers about who you are."

"What? What do you mean? Bagheera, come back! Ugh! I hate when you sneak off like that!"

Mowgli tried to keep up with his quick friend.

He clambered easily over rocks and swung on the low-hanging tree branches. But as fast as Mowgli was, he lost sight of Bagheera.

Then he spotted prints leading through the trees. His heart started thumping. These prints had five little toes, just like his!

He'd never seen paw prints like his before.

But he hadn't gone that way today. If they weren't his prints, whose were they?

One step at a time, Mowgli followed the strange prints.

chapter 2

Mowgli hopped from rock to rock, calling out greetings to familiar faces—a cheery gecko crawling up a trunk and a rhinoceros slowly lumbering through the trees—as he went. He kept his eyes on the prints, though.

Where did they lead?

After a while, he pulled back tree branches to peer into a small clearing. He spotted a bunch of curious dens, built from branches and tree limbs. There were tracks in the dirt outside them and piles of the little bones that all animals left behind after meals. Who lived here? Could it be the humans Bagheera spoke of?

Mowgli leaned out to take a better look and then gasped when a nose bumped against his neck.

"Jumpy, aren't you, little frog?"

"Viaan!" Mowgli was grateful to see his big brother. "I thought you went home."

"I turned around and saw you weren't with us. Mom thought we lost you somewhere." Viaan grunted. "What are you doing?"

"I want to see the flame flower," Mowgli whispered. "And humans, too. I've never seen one. Are they big? Are they hairy?"

"Father says they're very strange," Viaan said. As the second-oldest, he enjoyed when he could teach Mowgli something. "They walk on two legs instead of four, and they talk in this weird way—all tongue and no teeth. Mowgli, where are you going?"

Mowgli had crept out of the bushes and toward one of the human dens. "I want to see one," he whispered.

"Mowgli, come back!" Viaan howled after him, but Mowgli was already crouched in front of a den. He examined several large, round things that looked like river stones but were scooped out in the middle to make containers. Mowgli stuck his hand in one, then pulled it back out.

"Honey!" He licked it off his fingers. "Why is it inside a stone instead of in a beehive?"

"You shouldn't be touching the human

things." Viaan's nose twitched nervously. "I don't like this. I smell them nearby."

"We'll be quick." Mowgli poked around. Then something flickered in the corner of his eye. "Whoa! Is that…?"

He and Viaan crept toward a hole dug into the ground in front of the human den. Something bright and orange bloomed within it.

A flame flower!

"It's beautiful," Viaan whispered.

"Yes," Mowgli said softly. "I wonder what they use it for. Does it give nectar?"

He noticed smaller buds glowing around the larger flower. He tried to pick one up, not understanding that the flame flower was really fire.

"Oww!" he hissed, putting his fingers in his mouth. The flame flower burned.

He carefully pulled out a stick. A piece of the

flame flower burned brightly at its end. He rested it inside of one of the small stone pots.

"Why do you have that?" Viaan asked.

"I want to figure out why humans keep it." Mowgli balanced the stone on his hip. His hands were slippery and the stone slid between his fingers, so he put it back down for a moment to rub his hands on his legs. "It's so pretty. I want to grow one of my own."

Viaan's ears pricked, hearing something. "Let's go. Right now."

"Why?" Mowgli asked, but his brother had already raced off. And then, when he turned around, he saw why. Behind a tree stood what must be a young human.

For a moment, they just stared at each other. Mowgli couldn't believe what he was seeing. She looked like him, from her small fingers and toes

to her wide mouth, dark hair, and brown skin. How could this be possible?

Before Mowgli could say anything, there was a cry from another human den.

"Wolf! There's a wolf!"

The human girl whirled around, and Mowgli ran past her, still holding the pot. He ran for the bushes, not looking back.

"Wait!" she called after him. "Don't be afraid!"

But Mowgli didn't want to look back. Who was that? Why did Mowgli look so much like her, and like the humans rushing out of their dens?

Viaan was already far ahead of him and quickly disappeared into the trees. Mowgli ran as fast as he could, trying to keep the flame flower balanced without its sparks flying toward him.

He burst out of the bushes in front of their cave.

"Mowgli! Where have you been?" Raksha, Mowgli's mother, frowned at him. Her white-streaked fur bristled.

"Mother, I'm sorry but I—"

"Never mind that, sweetheart. You can't be here right now."

"Why not?" Mowgli asked. "What happened?"

Before his mother could say more, Mowgli heard his father, Akeela, growl in the distance.

"There's going to be a circle of the wolf elders," Raksha said hurriedly. "Stay here with the younger cubs."

"A circle?" Mowgli was confused. The wolf circles were the pack's monthly meetings. They usually happened on nights when the moon was full. Mowgli loved them because he got to stay up late and lean into his mother's warm, fuzzy side while his father and the other leaders of the pack talked about grown-up business. Once they were done, they all practiced their howls and sang the old, special songs about hunting.

"But I always get to join circles. And look, today I brought—"

"Mowgli, listen to me. You can't come this time." His mother's voice was firm. "Stay here, and don't leave until I come back."

Before Mowgli could argue, or show what he had, Raksha bounded off.

Mowgli stared after her, not even noticing one of his baby cousins stumbling over his feet. Then he spotted his oldest brother following their mother toward the clearing. "Wait! Sharaad, what's happening?"

Sharaad hesitated. "I think Father's in trouble."

"Why? Did something happen at the hunt?"

"I don't know, Mowgli, but I'll let you know what I find out. Later, all right?"

Mowgli watched his brother leave.

If Father's in trouble, Mowgli thought, *I have to find out what's happening in that circle.*

Mowgli quietly crept after his brother.

chapter 3

The entire wolf pack was gathered in an area of rough rock and sandy dirt. Mowgli crept through the bushes, hoping he wasn't close enough to be smelled.

A cold nose dug into his shoulder. "Mowgli! Mother told you to stay with the little cubs."

Sharaad shook his shaggy head.

Viaan sidled up to them. "You're both making a lot of noise," he hissed. "Is Mowgli staying?"

"No." Sharaad stuck out his tail and raised his chin. "He's going back where he will be safe."

"I'm safe here!" Mowgli tossed his hands up in frustration. "You guys are with me."

"He's right. Besides, he's always been big enough to join the circle before," Viaan said. "If we don't keep him with us, he'll just get into trouble."

Sharaad looked between his younger brothers. Mowgli tried to make his face innocent, and Sharaad snorted. "Okay, okay. But stay close. We need to keep Mother from seeing you, or we'll all be in for it."

Mowgli was relieved that, as always, his brothers were on his side. "How are we going to do that?"

Viaan hummed thoughtfully. "I have an idea."
He told his brothers his plan.

Mowgli placed the pot with the flame flower on the ground, then bent as low as possible and hid under the fluffy bellies of his older brothers.

"I can't believe we're doing this," Sharaad said in a low voice.

"Mother looks worried," Viaan whispered.

"I can't see," Mowgli muttered back.

The voices of the elder wolves were muffled, but Mowgli could tell they were arguing. He heard bits of what they were saying: "...not responsible" and "a bad look for the pack."

Then his father, Akeela, roared over all of them. "I know I failed at my hunt! I let the animal escape! I understand the pack is upset with me. You've said enough."

Mowgli gasped into his arm. His father had

failed at a hunt? He was the best, bravest, and strongest wolf in their pack. How could this happen?

Mowgli's mother spoke up. "If my husband failed, it is up to the pack to decide whether he should remain our leader. But why is that…that monster here?"

Mowgli tried to see through the tufts of fur in front of his eyes. "Who's here? What monster?"

"Stop wriggling, will you?" Sharaad whispered. "I can't see who it is, either."

At that moment, a low, chilling snarl sent a shiver down Mowgli's spine.

"It's Shere Khan!" Viaan cried.

Mowgli pushed his way forward to stare at the legendary Bengal tiger.

The big, striped cat tormented all who lived in the jungle. If a bird sat on too low a branch,

Shere Khan pounced for it. He'd rip off its beautiful feathers or crush its eggs in its nest, even if he wasn't hungry.

Many tigers were mean, but Shere Khan was downright awful. He wasn't welcome among the wolves.

Akeela growled. "Shere Khan. How dare you come here!"

"I wanted to watch the pack get rid of you. You are weak and old, Akeela. Your time is up."

Mowgli's brothers gasped, and Mowgli clapped a hand over his mouth. Before today, Shere Khan had never dared talk to Akeela like that. Even worse, behind him, the other members of the pack nodded.

"He may be right," one of them said. "We need a leader who can feed us."

"You do not get to decide who leads the

wolves," Mowgli's mother told Shere Khan.

"Calm yourself, Raksha. It's not Akeela I want. Well, at least not now. I'm here to settle an old debt. I want your child," said the tiger.

Everyone looked stunned.

"No," Raksha snarled.

"Protest all you want," Shere Khan sneered, "but I found that human child first, and you took him from me."

The words hit Mowgli like cold water on his head.

So it was true.

Once, Mowgli had overheard some other wolf parents discussing him. One of them had said, "It was lucky Mowgli's parents found him when they did."

"Did I ever get lost?" Mowgli had asked his mother later that day, and told her what he'd heard. She was quiet for a moment and then licked his head gently.

"Shere Khan chased away your first family," she'd said. "They are safe, but we do not know where they went. But that doesn't matter. You are our cub now."

So he was a human child?

In disbelief, he listened as Akeela roared, "Yes, our child! We took him in after you chased off his family and made them drop him. We claimed him and raised him. We protect him. If you dare try to harm him—"

Shere Khan's voice changed. Before, it was a purr, but now it grew louder and harsh. "Watch yourself, Akeela. You're getting older and weak. That's probably why you lost your hunt, isn't it? I may be as old as you, but I've kept myself strong. Also, don't forget that I'm doing the jungle a favor. Men don't belong here. They cut down the trees and their dreadful flame flowers burn down our homes. Why are you eager to protect one of them?"

Mowgli clenched his fists, hands trembling. Was all this true? Were men so bad? And if so, how could he possibly be one of them?

"Do not threaten my son," Mowgli's mother said. "I am warning you, Shere Khan!"

But the rest of the pack was murmuring.

"Men are harmful."

"That's right."

"Why not give Shere Khan what he wants?"

"Unbelievable," Sharaad muttered angrily. "If they think we'll give up our little brother…"

Mowgli stood, shaking from head to toe in anger. Viaan tried to press him back down with his paws. "What are you doing, Mowgli?"

"Shere Khan!" Mowgli hollered. Both his parents turned, wide-eyed.

Shere Khan slowly prowled toward him. The tiger was big, and his claws shone in the afternoon sunlight. It took all the courage and anger in Mowgli's heart to stand firm.

"So, it is true," the tiger growled. "The little human child I nearly captured is alive and well."

Raksha slid in front of Mowgli, teeth bared. "Step back, Shere Khan," she warned, "or you will regret it."

Shere Khan bared his own sharp teeth and snarled before springing forward.

Mowgli kicked the pot at his feet as he rushed in front of his mother. The flame flower spilled out, sparking to life. Shere Khan let out a yelp of pain as it lashed across his face. The tiger turned and ran into the bushes.

Mowgli watched, panting, as members of the pack hurriedly stamped on the flame flower, yelping as the heat burned their paws. They hurried to cool their burns in the nearby stream.

"That should scare him off our land now," Mowgli said proudly.

He expected the pack to thank him. Instead, they were angry.

"Where did you get that flame flower?" a wolf with pale gray fur howled.

"He must have gotten it from the human

dens!" cried another wolf, whisking his feathery tail.

"Is that true, Mowgli?" Mowgli's father asked, concerned. "Did you go there?"

"I did." Mowgli's lip trembled. "I was just curious."

"What can you expect from a human child?" a wolf mother, her neck hair long and shaggy over her shoulders, muttered. "We warned your parents you'd be trouble when they found you."

Mowgli looked at his parents. "Mother, was what Shere Khan said true? Am I one of those men?"

"Yes, my little frog. But you've always been a wolf, too. That is what matters most." Raksha lowered her head and shook it.

"But—"

She hurried over to him. "Shere Khan has seen

you, and he will keep returning to get you. You'll always be part of this family, but for now you cannot stay here. You need to go far away from us to be safe."

"Why do we need to send him away? We can protect him here," Sharaad cried.

"Yes," Viaan chimed in angrily. "We won't let Shere Khan threaten our little brother!"

"Your mother is right," Akeela said sadly. "Mowgli, the time has come for you to seek out the men. You look like one of them, and Shere Khan is scared of their sticks and flame flowers. Stay with them, and when it is safe, we will come for you."

Mowgli looked around the pack. Many of the wolves snarled at him.

"Go away."

"Leave us alone!"

His heart ached at their words. "No! I can't leave you."

"Go. Go now," Raksha licked his face, then nudged him forward. "Bagheera! Bagheera, I know you're here!"

"No need to shout." The panther's silky voice floated out from within the bushes. The big cat slowly emerged. "Don't worry, my friends. I'll watch over Mowgli until he arrives safely."

"Go now," Akeela said. "And be safe, our little frog."

Mowgli stared at his parents and his brothers. They nodded at him, their faces sad.

With tears streaming down his cheeks, Mowgli turned and ran into the trees. Bagheera hurried behind him, lifting Mowgli onto his back with a quick lash of his tail. Mowgli dug his fingers into the panther's soft, dark fur.

This must be a bad dream, he thought.

But it felt all too real.

chapter 4

"Ow!" Mowgli rolled over and was poked in the back by a branch.

He opened his eyes and sighed. He'd hoped to wake up safe and snuggled between his sleeping brothers, warm in their fur. Instead, he was exactly where he was the night before.

Out in the middle of the jungle.

Chased off by his own pack.

Twigs and branches from the tent he'd made tumbled onto his head. Mowgli gave a sniff and rubbed his arm across his nose.

"Why the long face, friend?" a voice chittered overhead.

"Yeah, why so sad?" called another voice.

Mowgli looked up. "Who's there?"

"Oh, everyone."

"And no one."

"Just us, you see. The monkeys!"

Sure enough, several little monkeys with wide grins peered down at him from the trees. They dangled on matted, wildly spiked tails. Mowgli had seen them swinging through the treetops and nibbling on sweet bananas. He'd wanted to play with them, but his mother disapproved. She called them "little troublemakers."

Mowgli felt a pang in his heart at the thought of his parents, then shook it away. They weren't here now. *They* told him to leave. They didn't have a right to decide what he did anymore.

As soon as he thought that, he felt ashamed. No. Being mad at his parents wasn't the answer. This was Shere Khan's fault.

"Cheer up!" one of the monkeys chirped, handing him a ripe mango. Mowgli was surprised and a little pleased to have someone looking out for him.

"Yeah! Cheer up!" called another monkey. "We think you're cool!"

"How did you make that log cave? Looks quite snuggly—eek!" The first monkey nearly toppled out of the tree as a large, furry brown paw knocked the trunk.

"Oops." A shaggy sloth bear lumbered into view. "I must have slipped."

"Baloo!" Mowgli exclaimed happily. "Why are you here, too?"

Along with Bagheera, Baloo was Mowgli's other best friend. Baloo scratched his round belly.

"Bagheera was worried about you wandering off," he explained, patting Mowgli's head. "I showed up while you were sleeping last night. He left me to watch you until he gets back."

"Bagheera shouldn't worry," Mowgli said, but he was secretly glad his friends were with him. "I'm fine. Don't you have better things to do?"

"Good friends never leave you alone," Bagheera called from behind them. The panther sauntered up and carefully dropped a banana from between his teeth. "Eat that. You're a growing cub. Now, why were you talking to the monkeys?"

"They seem nice," Mowgli said, breaking off a chunk of the banana and walking with his friends. "They gave me this mango."

Baloo sniffed. "They seem nice for now. Just you wait. Listen, Mowgli. We've taught you a lot about the ways of the jungle, right?"

"Right!"

"And we've never steered you wrong, right?"

"Of course!" Mowgli said firmly. "You've been

my teachers for years. You guys know everything about the jungle."

"That's right." Bagheera purred proudly.

Baloo split open the mango with his long claws. "We've told you the ways to greet others in the jungle, yes?"

Mowgli furrowed his brow thoughtfully. "You taught me how to call hello to the birds, but…I forget the exact sound."

Bagheera let out a high chirrup. A great bird of paradise trilled back and spread its wings on an overhead branch.

"May the air carry you like a feather and your nest be safe," Bagheera said to the bird.

"Good morning, brother," it called down.

"It doesn't matter if you know the right word or not, as long as you're polite. Your mother told you that, yes?" asked Bagheera.

Mowgli lowered his head sadly. "She did."

Raksha made sure her cubs were the best behaved in the pack. The thought of his mother roughly patting his back with her paw and sighing about how naughty her little frog was made Mowgli's eyes prickle all over again.

"No tears," Baloo said hurriedly. "Bagheera, show him how you greet the snakes!"

Bagheera quickly stuck out his long pink tongue.

"That looks so silly, Bagheera!" Mowgli giggled.

"Not if you're a snake," Bagheera replied. "Be careful to show your whole tongue and not only the tip. If it's just the tip, you're laughing at them."

"Got it." A tickle on Mowgli's foot startled him, and he looked down at a mouse climbing over it. He lifted it into his hands. "What about this mouse? How do I greet it?"

As Bagheera started to answer, the monkeys above them began to chitter and giggle.

"Is that what you're going to do all day?"

"So boring!"

"Let's do something fun!"

One of the monkeys dropped onto a branch and did a headstand. "Like this, panther! Do this!"

"You know very well I can't," Bagheera said tiredly. "And I'm not here to entertain you. Why don't you do something useful, like collect fruit, instead of your silly monkey business?"

The monkey sniffed. "That sounds *bo-rrring*."

"Besides," another chimed in, "the human child is more interesting."

"We want to play with him!"

"The human child has no time to play with you," Baloo insisted. "We need to make sure he gets to the human dens before dark. Go on, now."

The monkeys chittered unhappily.

"No, no, no! We want him to play with us now!"

"Come, human child! Swing with us!"

Before Bagheera could say anything more or Baloo could use one of his large paws, two monkeys reached down and snatched Mowgli up into the treetops. They tossed him from monkey to monkey. Mowgli flew through the air from one wiry set of arms to another.

"See?" one monkey cried. "It's like you're a bird!"

Mowgli laughed happily. The sun shone warm on his face and back. When he looked down, the jungle was spread out all bright and green and beautiful.

"Okay," he said after a while. "This was fun. You can put me down. I'm getting a little dizzy."

"But we've only just started playing!" the monkeys protested.

"But I want to be put down," Mowgli insisted. "When someone is done playing, you stop."

"Not until you've seen our home!"

"Yes! Yes, let us show you our home, human child!"

"Baloo!" Mowgli cried out. "Bagheera!"

He heard Bagheera's and Baloo's worried voices far below, but they soon faded away. Air rushed past Mowgli's ears and whipped tears into his eyes. All he could do was wait as the monkeys carried him far, far away.

chapter 5

The monkeys carried Mowgli through the branches. His head spun and his stomach lurched. He kept his eyes squeezed shut so he didn't have to see the ground moving rapidly beneath him.

"Where are you taking me?" he called out.

"We already told you," a monkey chittered back. "To our home! Don't worry!"

Mowgli squeezed his eyes tighter. He hung on and hoped the crazy ride would stop soon.

And then it did.

"Open your eyes, human child!"

"Yes, yes, yes! Open them!"

Mowgli cautiously opened one eye, then the other. He couldn't believe what he was seeing. "Wow. What is this place?"

It looked like one of the human dens, only much bigger. The walls and the floor were carved from shiny gray stone. There had been a roof at one point, but it had fallen in.

"This," a monkey said grandly, sweeping out its skinny arm, "is the hidden City of the Monkey King."

"You have a king?"

"We used to. And then he got boring."

Thick vines grew over the floor, and Mowgli saw little puddles from the last rainstorm. Tiny, dark figures darted across the surface.

"Tadpoles," he whispered, and felt a little better. Even if he wasn't a frog, it was nice to see something familiar.

"Like it, do you?" one of the monkeys asked.

"It's cool, right?"

"And all of it is yours now!"

Mowgli took a step back. "Wait. Mine?"

"Yes! We finally have a new king!" cried the monkeys. They grabbed him up and danced with him, spinning him around.

"Whoa! I'm getting dizzy again," Mowgli warned. "And what do you mean, king? Why am I your king?"

"You do such clever things," said one monkey.

"You build dens out of sticks, and even grumpy old Bagheera listens to you."

"He would listen to you, too, if you didn't call him grumpy," Mowgli said, but the monkeys weren't listening.

"Hooray! Hooray! We have a king! And now it's time to feast. Eat up, our king! Eat up!"

Mowgli found himself being led to a big stone chair. It was hard and uncomfortable, but he liked the fancy pictures carved into its arms of monkeys dancing around a large tree. The monkeys surrounded him, fanning him with big leaves. He was fed ripe mangoes and sweet grapes.

Mowgli shifted in his seat, trying to figure out what to do. The monkeys didn't seem bad, but he didn't want to stay here. As he sat, he felt something smooth and cold slither over his foot.

"Oh, it is those snakes!" The monkeys started

shrieking. "We don't like those at all."

A long, skinny python wrapped itself around Mowgli's leg. Mowgli swallowed hard and then stuck out his tongue. "Hello, snake brother," he said in as good a hiss as he could manage.

"Hello," the snake hissed back. "Are you the human child of the wolf pack?"

"Yes! Yes, I am!" cried Mowgli.

"You are welcome here. Just be careful. We like to slide over the floor."

"I understand," Mowgli said, and patted the snake on its head. The monkeys watched in awe.

The monkeys were impressed by everything Mowgli did. He built his small stick dens, and they all chittered and clapped.

"Another trick, our king!" they chanted. "Another trick!"

He reached into one of the small streams that trailed across the floor and caught a tiny fish between his fingers.

"Wow! Wow!" the monkeys cried. "Please teach us your marvelous ways!"

Mowgli tried. He really did. But the monkeys were not good students. They wanted him to build their stick dens and catch their fish for them, instead of learning for themselves.

"The sticks are too sharp, and they poke me!" one monkey complained.

Another said, "Working is no fun. Let's play."

They threw dirt and nuts. They laughed and shrieked when Mowgli splashed his face in the stream. They didn't believe in taking baths.

"You'll only get dirty again!" they screamed. "Silly human child!"

They didn't have any rules, except one: everything had to be fun, or else they threw it away.

One night, after they served him a fruit dinner fit for a king, Mowgli announced, "I'm leaving in the morning to find my friends."

The monkeys jumped up and down frantically, pinching his arm. "No! No! You're ours now!"

"Ow! It isn't nice to do that," Mowgli said.

"You can't leave yet," the monkeys insisted. "You still need to help us grow a flame flower."

Mowgli looked at them, confused. "A flame flower? I don't know how to grow one of those."

"Sure you can! You're a human child, aren't you?"

"No," Mowgli said firmly. "I'm not. Well, I am in a way, but I'm also a jungle child, just like you guys."

"Whatever." The monkeys waved him off. "We heard you had a flame flower. That's why we chose you as our king."

"Yeah, and you burned Shere Khan with it!"

"So now you have to share it with us!"

Mowgli walked away, shaking his head as they argued over whether they could share a flame flower and who deserved it most. He missed his pack, where the little pups might sometimes be annoying but listened to their big brothers and sisters and cousins. They were loud only when they were laughing. The monkeys were always loud but never happy.

Even if he could give them a flame flower, he was sure they'd find it boring soon.

He needed to figure out a way to escape the City of the Monkey King. The monkeys blocked the doors and surrounded him whenever he moved. They lay around him at night as he slept, and if he ever inched toward the exit, one of them would screech and then all of them would hold him down in a great big hug.

It was almost like one of Baloo's bear hugs, but more frustrating because…well, it wasn't a hug from Baloo.

But how was he supposed to leave without their noticing?

Then, as he stepped carefully over the small snakes darting in and out of the floor, he had an idea. He leaned down and hissed quietly, "Friends! Friends! Can you help me?"

One small snake stopped. "We will always help you, kind human child."

"Do you know Baloo the bear and Bagheera the panther?"

"I do not know them well, but our queen, Kaa, will know them. She is friends with all the important animals of the jungle!" the snake said eagerly.

"Please have Kaa tell them where I am," Mowgli whispered. "And tell them I need help."

The snake slithered off and Mowgli watched it go.

Would it be able to find his friends?

chapter 6

"How do you feed a flame flower?" the monkeys asked eagerly as he tried to eat breakfast the next morning. "Fresh eggs? Pollen?"

"Does it need to be planted in soil?" Another monkey scampered after Mowgli as he stepped on loose spots on the floor and tugged at vines to see if exits were hidden behind them.

Maybe if I'm quick enough and there's a tunnel, I could crawl through, Mowgli thought. He was pretty sure the monkeys, as much as they loved dirt, would get tired of following him.

But there weren't any tunnels. And their questions got more annoying.

"Is it true that it has teeth that can bite you?" asked a tiny monkey.

"What? No," Mowgli said. "It's not that kind of flower."

"A flower, a flower, a pretty, pretty flower!" The monkeys laughed and danced together. "We have our little human child king. Now we will have a party!"

Mowgli was startled. "What party?"

"We're going to crown you our king tonight!" one monkey said eagerly. "We'll have a special party, because you're the bravest, strongest, and fastest king there is! Only the best for us monkeys!"

Mowgli took a careful step backward. "We don't need to have a party."

"Yes, yes, yes!" They chittered and jumped up and down. "A party and a flame flower, too!"

Mowgli was swept up in a rush of hairy bodies and clingy hands and carried from the corner of the room back toward his stone throne. It took a few minutes for him to fight his way out.

"Wait. None of you even asked me if I want to be king. And I don't!" He stood with his arms crossed over his chest.

"Why not?" the monkeys asked.

"After all, we're quite fun to be with!"

"And we're doing you an honor, especially since you don't have fur!"

"I won't be your king!" Mowgli cried. "And I can't get you a flame flower."

The monkeys bristled with anger. They hopped up and down. "What? Really? You insult us after all we did for you?"

"We'll make you give us a flame flower."

The monkeys tugged at his hair and yelled in his ears.

"Stop that!" Mowgli tried to slide out of their grasps, toward the wall. They closed in. Closer and closer. Mowgli gulped nervously.

"Snake friends!" he hissed desperately.

"We're here," the snakes hissed from under his feet. They started tangling themselves around the monkeys' paws.

The monkeys screeched in fear. They tried to shake the scaly creatures off.

"Bird friends!" Mowgli chirped desperately toward the roof. He'd seen little nests up there.

"We're here, human child," a voice cawed. The birds pelted nuts and seeds at the monkeys' heads.

"No fair!" the monkeys cried. "Ow! Stop that, stop that!"

"Yes! Stop that!" a familiar deep voice bellowed.

Mowgli turned. "Baloo! Bagheera!"

He threw himself at Baloo's furry legs, hugging them, and then reached out to scratch behind Bagheera's ears. The familiar feel of the silky fur made him laugh happily. His friends were here. Everything would be okay.

"Are you all right?" Bagheera purred and licked his face.

"Yes," Mowgli said bravely. "How did you get here?"

"I brought them," a voice hissed beneath his feet.

Kaa, an enormous Indian rock python, slithered past the other snakes, who bowed their heads in greeting. Mowgli bowed his head, too, even though he didn't want to take his eyes off Kaa. Her tan skin had wide brown splotches. She was both beautiful and terrifying.

"We came through a tunnel that leads through the back wall," said Kaa.

"Ah!" Mowgli gasped excitedly. There *were* tunnels!

"Go now, Mowgli. We'll take care of the monkeys." Kaa pulled her neck up and opened her mouth as wide as it could go.

The monkeys were terrified. "Kaa will choke us and swallow us!"

The monkeys ran back and forth, panicked and chittering. A few leaped onto the stone throne, and others climbed up the walls. Some managed to get into the trees that hung over the ruined walls. The rest only stared at Kaa in fear.

"I am very angry with you monkeys," Kaa hissed, her head waving to and fro. "You've been warned not to cause trouble. Now I'm going to squeeze you. And while I squeeze you, you will think about how you will apologize to Mowgli later."

"We can apologize now!" they jabbered. "Really, we can!"

"Later. Mowgli must go to the human dens now."

Baloo lifted Mowgli onto Bagheera's back. Mowgli closed his eyes as Bagheera took off.

"Duck," Bagheera grunted as they entered the tunnel. Stone scraped Mowgli's hands and Bagheera's sides. Within moments, they were back outside. Mowgli smelled the low-hanging berries and sharpness of tree sap as branches whipped past his face. He heard Baloo lumbering behind them, snuffling softly through his nose.

It was a long time before Bagheera stopped, and Baloo gently lifted Mowgli off.

Mowgli looked around nervously. They stood

in a large dirt clearing at the edge of the jungle. A fence made of chopped wood surrounded many human dens, and little pits held flame flowers. He picked up many new smells, but some of them—fragrant crushed pepper and a hint of squeezed lemon—were familiar.

Bagheera licked Mowgli's chin, and Baloo ruffled his messy hair.

"We'll always be near, if you call for us," Bagheera said. "Be brave, little frog. Be brave."

Mowgli watched his friends melt back into the green jungle.

Then Mowgli took a deep breath and turned to face the man village.

chapter 7

Mowgli decided he'd slip into the village the same way he'd introduce himself into an unfamiliar wolf pack. The trick was to keep his head down and stay as quiet as possible. The pack would politely turn their heads away until the guest was examined and sniffed by the pack's leader. Once the guest passed the leader's test, he'd be a friend to everyone as long as he followed the rules. Mowgli hoped that men worked the same way as wolves.

But as soon as he stepped into the village, he was surrounded. Fingers prodded his arms and tugged at his mouth to check his teeth. They grabbed tufts of his shaggy hair.

"Whose strange child is this?" an old man asked.

"Look at his arms," someone called. "See those scars?"

"He smells like a wolf," a woman said. "I don't like this at all."

Mowgli growled. They all gasped and backed away.

"This is definitely a wolf child," declared the old man.

"Send him back into the jungle!" someone

called out in a terrified voice. "If he stays here, the wolves will come and eat all our food."

"They will bring their friends, too!"

Mowgli tried to back up toward the forest as the yelling and poking continued, but the crowd was too strong. He was carried deeper into the village and sat down in front of a flame flower between two human dens.

"If we let him go now," one man announced, "he'll tell them exactly how to find us and steal our dinner."

"But he can't stay here," someone else protested. "He might be dangerous himself!"

The man language moved fast like a sleek snake between the people speaking. Perhaps it was the disgusted looks on their faces or the way someone reached out to tug at his lip, but he understood he wasn't wanted.

He stood, and they made even more noise.

"Sit right there where we can see you!"

"No, send him back where he belongs," one woman said, her arms crossed over her chest. "If his friends come here, we can chase them off, too."

"No, no! Wait!" A beautiful woman in a yellow patterned sari and with long black hair flowing down her back rushed over. Mowgli stiffened in surprise as she threw her arms around him.

"My son! You've come back to me!"

Son?

Mowgli tried to draw his head back so he could see her properly. She smelled like the best type of tree bark: the spicy brown kind that Mowgli's wolf mother tugged back with her sharp teeth and used to make their den smell nice.

Could this woman really be his human mother?

The woman turned and faced the crowd. "My baby son was lost in the jungle several years ago—don't you remember? My husband and I lost him while trying to escape the tiger. And now my boy has come back!"

The warmth of her and the sweetness to her voice reminded Mowgli of Raksha. He leaned into her. She wrapped an arm around his shoulder.

A man behind her cleared his throat tentatively. "Shamima, it's been years. How do you know this is your son?"

"It could be a trick." An old man eyed Mowgli with suspicion. "You can't trust the jungle, or anyone who comes out of it."

Mowgli scowled. He didn't like this old man at all.

But another man stepped up and put his hand on the woman's shoulder. "I stand by my wife

and my son. If anyone has a problem with that, I'm happy to leave the village with them, but I'm the best businessman you have. If we leave, you may have trouble trading crops with the other villages."

The crowd quieted. Mowgli eyed the man with interest. He seemed to be as powerful as Mowgli's dad Akeela was in their pack.

"There's no need for that, Pavesh," the old man spluttered. "I'm glad your son has come back to you, too."

The woman smiled down at Mowgli and hugged him tighter. The man ruffled his hair. Mowgli didn't quite know what was going on, but he smiled back.

Maybe this wouldn't be so bad.

chapter 8

Life in the village was strange.

Mowgli's mother, Shamima, was sweet and taught him the words he needed to learn his new language. There was so much to remember and do the right way, from sleeping inside to wearing clothes.

"A boy like you shouldn't be running around in leaves and dirty cloth," Shamima scolded as he backed away into a corner of the house. That was what you called a human den, he'd found out: a house. "Don't you think these clothes I picked out for you look nice?"

Mowgli glanced at the itchy short-sleeved shirt and embroidered drawstring shorts. They didn't look nice at all. But before Mowgli could protest, the shirt was slipped over his head.

"How handsome! Don't you feel better now?" Shamima's eyes shone and she hugged him tightly, so he didn't complain.

Shamima and Pavesh made him eat with his fingers instead of bending down and slurping the food into his mouth. They made him go in and out the door instead of climbing through the windows.

Mowgli tried. He really did.

But when the other kids laughed at the growl that worked its way into his voice when he spoke, he couldn't hide his hurt. When he first saw the kids, he'd been excited. They had the same smooth brown skin and thin legs as he did. But instead of wrestling and practicing their biting like the wolf pack did, they sat in a circle at school. They spent a lot of time drawing with long, thin sticks.

They also spent a lot of time making fun of Mowgli.

"Your tongue sticks out just like a wolf," a girl would say with a frown when he tried to practice a new word, like *book* or *shoes*.

When Mowgli rubbed his nose against a new friend's face to say thank you, the boy would pull away with wide eyes.

"Only wolves would do that!" he exclaimed.

"What's wrong with being like a wolf?" Mowgli asked.

"It's not like a man," the boy tried to explain. "It's too much like the jungle."

"But I'm a jungle child," Mowgli said.

Pavesh and Shamima didn't like to hear that. "Now that you're back with us, you need to remember who you are. You are a wonderful, strong *human* child."

"I can be a human child and a jungle child," Mowgli insisted.

But his parents just looked at each other and shook their heads.

Shamima seemed eager to keep Mowgli away from the jungle. Every time he looked toward the trees, her eyes filled with tears.

"Are you unhappy here?" she'd ask. "Should

I make something different for you to eat, or weave a softer blanket for your bed? Tell me how to make you happy."

Mowgli would hug her and tell her that she was doing everything right for him. And it was true. He could tell that his father and mother were very good people, and they loved him and had missed him a lot.

He just wished that it was easier to enjoy the life in the quiet village they seemed to like so much. They didn't seem to feel uncomfortable in their clothes. They didn't want to explore the jungle and all the marvelous things that could be found in it.

"The jungle is horrible," Shamima said one day when Mowgli tried to ask her about it. "There are dangerous things in there."

Pavesh shook his head. "This is where men need to be, Mowgli. Here."

So Mowgli went to the school and learned to pull his tongue in. He made Shamima happy by sleeping in his bed instead of on the floor. But he couldn't stop feeling restless.

Pavesh was eager to find a way for him to fit in. "Everyone here has a job, and I want you to have one, too."

Everyone in the pack also had a job. Some wolves kept the dens clean. Others hunted to feed the group. But human jobs were a whole lot trickier than wolf jobs. And there were a lot more of them, from washing clothes to patching up holes in the human den walls.

At first, no one wanted to give Mowgli a job. Mowgli knew it was because the village elders didn't like him. Even though he wore clothes now and ate politely with one hand instead of two, they eyed him suspiciously. When he walked by and said hello, they never responded. Instead, they waited until he passed to keep whispering about him.

But one day, Pavesh finally came home with a job for Mowgli.

"We need someone to herd the cows," Pavesh said cheerfully. "Mowgli, you should be good at that. Animals like you."

"Cow herding?" he complained as Shamima worked oil into his stubborn hair. "Can't I do something else?"

Cows were nice enough, he guessed. He knew how to greet them. But they only wanted to talk about the weather. Or how delicious grass was. Mowgli had tried grass. It wasn't all that delicious. And talking about weather got old really, really quickly.

"This is a good job to start," Pavesh said.

Shamima agreed, though she added, "Be

careful to thank the elders for giving you this chance. And make sure to smile. They're still unsure about you."

Mowgli went out the next morning with fruit and bread in his bag and a stick in his hand. The cows trailed behind him. They were wary at first after smelling the wolves on him, but they liked him. All animals did—except Shere Khan.

"How's the weather?" one mooed in his ear.

Mowgli sighed. "It's very nice."

After lessons, he'd go out to take care of the cows, and sometimes kids from school would follow him. At first, it was just to make fun of him. But then they saw how the animals came to visit him. They watched him coax beautiful birds out of the trees and onto his arms. They noticed a little shrew run up his leg and hide behind his knee.

"How do you do that? They're not scared of you at all," they said.

"I know their names, and how to say hi."

Mowgli remembered Bagheera and Baloo's lessons about being kind and thoughtful when speaking with other animals. He missed his friends so much.

He had seen Bagheera once or twice, but from a careful distance. One day, he'd felt the hairs on the back of his neck rise as he sat in school. He turned his head toward the window and spotted Bagheera standing where the jungle trees met the clear area of the village.

Mowgli stood up from his seat so quickly that it

clattered to the floor. Everyone turned and stared.

The teacher frowned. "Is everything all right, Mowgli?"

Mowgli looked out the open window, but Bagheera was gone. Mowgli sighed and sat back down.

"I'm sorry, Teacher. I thought I saw a friend."

The teacher shook his head and continued his lesson.

Mowgli's wolf brothers visited often as the months passed. They'd wait until the cows were a little bit away and Mowgli was stretched out and eating his lunch alone in the pasture. Then they would curl up at his feet.

"How are Mother and Father?" Mowgli would ask eagerly. "And Baloo and Bagheera? Are the new pups walking yet?"

Viaan and Sharaad answered as best they

could, but never with the answer that Mowgli really wanted to hear: that it was safe for him to come home.

"Today?" he'd ask hopefully. Sharaad would shake his head, and Viaan would nuzzle his neck comfortingly.

"Soon, little frog," they both said.

But soon didn't seem to be coming fast enough.

So one year passed. And then another.

One day in the third year of his life in the village, Mowgli sat with his arms wrapped around his legs and watched the cows peacefully graze. Sometimes they would start chatting about how sunny it was or how nice the grass tasted, and he

would respond politely. He was homesick, thinking about his wolf family wrestling and tumbling and wandering through the jungle. He wanted to be with them.

But then he felt guilty.

Shamima and Pavesh had done so much for him. How could he be bored with village life when there was so much to learn: new words, new ways of doing things, new adventures?

Every time his wolf brothers visited, he told them about his new life. But they didn't think it was so exciting.

"Must you always go on about human ways?" Sharaad asked. "I'm worried about your voice. You're losing the wolf slide to your tongue in your words. Practice your growls and barks so you don't forget them entirely."

Mowgli was frustrated. What was wrong

with learning human words and human talk? He wouldn't lose his wolf tongue that easily. His brothers knew him better than that.

But when he protested, Viaan only shook his head. "You're already losing your tribe scent," he said sadly. "You smell like a human. I don't like it, Mowgli."

Mowgli sniffed his arm and tugged his hair to his nose. He didn't smell anything different.

"It's not Mowgli's fault," said Sharaad, trying to comfort both his brothers. "Once he comes home, he'll get his smell back."

"But when will that be?" Mowgli asked for what felt like the hundredth time.

"Soon, little frog," Sharaad said. "Just don't forget who you are while you wait."

Now Mowgli lay in the pasture and thought about his brothers. He missed the pack every single day. Then he heard a movement in the grass. Mowgli spotted Viaan rushing to greet him. Mowgli stood and waved happily.

Suddenly, a cry rang out behind him. "Mowgli! Watch out! Wolf!"

Mowgli whirled around. Shamima stood with her hands clasped over her heart. Behind her, several villagers holding large sticks hurried toward the pasture.

Viaan kept running forward. In an instant, Mowgli realized what was about to happen. The men see only a wolf. They don't know this is my brother.

He waved his arms at them. "No, no! You don't understand!"

The villagers didn't stop. They ran faster to help him. Mowgli's heart lurched. He couldn't let them hurt his brother.

He turned and waved his arms at Viaan this time. "Get back!" he hollered.

His brother froze. For a moment, there was utter silence as they locked eyes.

"Mowgli!" Shamima wailed behind him. "Run away from the wolf! What are you doing?"

Mowgli heard the pounding footsteps of the approaching men. He had to get his brother out of here—before they hurt him. He didn't have time to explain it to Viaan.

"Go!" Mowgli cried.

Viaan stared, utterly confused. His tongue still hung out the side of his mouth in happiness at seeing his little brother.

Mowgli panicked. He reached down and pulled off one of his new, uncomfortable sandals. He hurled it at his brother, who danced back.

"What are you doing?" Viaan yelped.

"Get away from me!" Mowgli cried. "Go! I don't want you here. You need to go—now!"

Puzzlement, then hurt, filled Viaan's eyes. He turned and bolted back into the jungle.

Mowgli dropped heavily to the ground, trying to catch his breath.

What did I just do?

chapter 9

That night, Mowgli sat cross-legged in front of the household fire. He now knew this was the proper word for a flame flower. Shamima fed him rice and vegetables, fussing in between every bite.

"What if something had happened to you?

What if that wolf had spun around and attacked you?"

I almost wish he had, Mowgli thought glumly. His brother hadn't said a word, only looked at him before running off. Guilt squirmed in his stomach. He knew what Bagheera would say.

You didn't need to do that, Mowgli.

Baloo would shake his head while peeling a mango with his claws. *What else could he do, Bagheera? His brother would have gotten hurt.*

I know that, the Bagheera in Mowgli's imagination huffed. *And I don't blame you, little frog. Really. But are you surprised your brother was upset? He thinks you chose the men over him.*

Mowgli's thoughts were interrupted by the door banging open. Pavesh stood there, his smile stretching from ear to ear. "Mowgli, the bonfire's starting. They want you to join."

Mowgli gasped. "Really? You mean it?"

The bonfire was like the wolf pack circles. Mowgli missed the circles, where everyone but the little pups was welcome. The bonfire, though, was only for "hard workers." The elders decided who could come. Being invited meant Mowgli had finally worked hard enough.

Pavesh walked him outside, an arm proudly around his shoulders. The villagers around the fire waved to him, calling out cheerfully, "Here's our little hero!" He was offered a plate of food: the flatbread, lentils, and leafy vegetables he'd grown used to.

The attention felt so nice. But Mowgli couldn't entirely enjoy it—not when it came at the cost of his friendship with his brother. He had to make it up to Viaan. But how?

As they ate and drank, he listened to the villagers talk.

"That horrible, mean panther scared my

chickens again," one woman grumbled. "Now they won't lay eggs."

"What about that hideous bear?" Another woman leaned in. "It lumbered by and frightened my children the other day."

They were talking about Bagheera and Baloo! But his friends weren't mean or scary.

He stared in disbelief. How could they be so afraid? Bagheera and Baloo were probably prowling around the village to check on him. They weren't dangerous.

"Did they hurt you in any way?" Mowgli asked.

"Well, no," the first woman said slowly. "But they could have! You never know."

"Neither of them are half as fierce as that tiger," one of the village elders said, leaning down to take a sweet off a plate.

The men around Mowgli all nodded.

Mowgli was shocked. "Are you talking about Shere Khan?"

"Is that what you call him?" the elder asked. "The old tiger knocks down our houses and chases our children. I may hate him, but he is stronger and cleverer than any other animal."

Mowgli couldn't believe his ears. How could they praise that horrible tiger?

He jumped up, fists clenched. "Shere Khan is terrible! That old tiger was the reason my parents dropped me and lost me in the jungle. He has scared and hunted so many animals. What good is there in Shere Khan?"

"Watch what you say, boy," warned a man with a thick black beard. "If you keep calling him, you will bring the tiger here, and then what will you do?"

"Let him come!" Mowgli said bravely. "I'm not scared of Shere Khan."

Suddenly a woman screamed. In the trees surrounding the bonfire, two large yellow eyes flashed. The villagers sprang up, grabbing their children and racing toward their homes.

Mowgli stood frozen, watching the yellow eyes draw closer, his heart in his throat. Was it Shere Khan? He wished he had a stick or something to scare off the tiger. He swallowed hard and tried to stand tall, but his knees trembled.

Why did I have to blurt out Shere Khan's name like that?

The firelight illuminated a furry face. Mowgli squinted and saw a long snout and two pointed ears.

"Sharaad!" Mowgli launched himself at his older brother and wrapped his arms around his

neck. Sharaad licked his face. "Oh, Sharaad, I'm
so glad to see you! Is Viaan angry with me?"

"No, he understands. Listen, I don't have

much time. I raced here to tell you the news. Shere Khan knows you're in the human village. He's hunting for you."

Sharaad turned back toward the trees. Mowgli stretched out his hand. "Wait, that's it? Sharaad, what do I do?"

"You have to be strong, Mowgli," Sharaad said.

"By myself?"

"I need to get the cubs to safety, but I'll be back as soon as I can. Bagheera and Baloo are near. Be strong and be safe, little frog."

"Wait!"

But his brother was gone. Mowgli was alone.

chapter 10

What should I do? How do I defeat the tiger?" Mowgli paced back and forth in front of his house.

"Come inside, Mowgli," Shamima said anxiously from the window. She glanced past Mowgli to her husband. "Pavesh is mending the fence and then we will leave."

"But we need to get ready to fight Shere Khan," said Mowgli.

The woman next door stuck her head out her window. "Boy, don't be foolish. That tiger is stronger and faster than us all. We must go to one of the the village elders' big houses and stay in hiding until he moves on."

Mowgli refused to hide. Everyone else could. There'd be plenty of guards and fire to scare the tiger away from the elder's home. He would face Shere Khan on his own.

Mowgli came up with a plan. He wasn't sure if it would work, but he had to try. If he didn't stand up to Shere Khan, he'd be looking over his shoulder forever.

"You two go," Mowgli told Shamima and Pavesh a little later. Shamima froze outside the door with her best cooking pot on her hip. It was filled with the last of her bread to share with the others hiding in the village elder's house.

"What are you saying, Mowgli?" Pavesh asked. "You can't stay here with Shere Khan coming."

"This is what I need to do," Mowgli said stubbornly. "I need to fight Shere Khan."

Shamima dropped her pot on the floor and her hands flew up to her face. "Pavesh! What is this boy saying?"

Pavesh's voice was stern. "Mowgli, I know you're upset. You'll get hurt. We always hide when the tiger comes."

"Everyone leaves and hides, and Shere Khan messes up their homes and digs up their gardens. It must stop," Mowgli said.

"He took you away from me once. I don't want him to take you from me again." Shamima's eyes were wide and filled with tears.

Mowgli felt guilty, but he knew Shere Khan would keep coming back again and again to cause trouble—and to find Mowgli.

The sound of a loud horn trumpeted over the village. A moment later, the village elder called loudly, "Please, hurry inside my house now so we can close the gates!"

Pavesh steered tearful Shamima out the door. "The boy will leave if he sees us leaving. Mowgli, come with us and don't worry your mother."

Mowgli stayed put. He wasn't going to follow them. He had a job to do.

The village was quiet after everyone cleared out. Mowgli went to work. He dug an enormous hole near the cows' pasture. Bagheera had taught him how to make this simple trap. He covered the hole with large leaves so it looked like any other patch of ground. As the afternoon sun started to sink, he gathered the herd. He clucked at the cows to follow him.

"Now," Mowgli said firmly. "Now we will see what Shere Khan does."

As the cows wandered into the pasture, Mowgli stretched out on the soft grass. He closed his eyes and pretended to sleep. He wanted to draw the tiger to him. He listened carefully, knowing the tiger moved silently.

And then he heard it: the crack of a twig.

He sniffed and caught Shere Khan's scent. Mowgli's entire body stiffened, but he didn't dare move. He waited.

All was silent. Where was the tiger?

He waited. And waited.

Slowly, Mowgli cracked open one eye, then the other. He sat up.

There was a sudden snarl—and Mowgli was

tackled by a heavy mass of fur and bared claws. Shere Khan hadn't fallen for his trick after all!

"You!" Shere Khan growled down into his terrified face. "I'd wanted to give the human village trouble, but this is even better. You escaped me before, but you won't escape me today!"

Mowgli gritted his teeth and kicked out. His feet caught the tiger in the belly and, with a grunt, Shere Khan slid back on his paws. Mowgli clambered to his feet, reaching for the stick he used to herd the cows. Shere Khan was faster, knocking the stick out of his grasp.

"What now, little frog?" He laughed. "What tricks do you have up your sleeve? Let me tell you, they will not work. I am old and clever and know exactly how to escape."

His paw flew out again, but this time Mowgli kicked it neatly, throwing Shere Khan off balance.

The tiger howled and toppled backward—

Right into the enormous hole.

For a moment, there was no sound except for Mowgli's panting. He waited to hear a roar or a growl.

The tiger was completely silent.

Have I really taken down the powerful Shere Khan?

chapter 11

Mowgli tiptoed to the edge of the hole and stared down.

Below, Shere Khan snarled and snapped his teeth. He tried to pounce upward. Mowgli cringed, shielding his face with his hands. But the tiger's paws slipped on the damp earth, and he tumbled back into the hole.

"Let me out," he roared.

Mowgli sat on the ground in a daze. *I did it. I really did it,* he thought. *Shere Khan is trapped in the hole. And he can't get out.*

He'd caught the famous tiger that everyone in the jungle feared.

Mowgli jumped up and crowed a victory song. He laughed and danced from foot to foot. "I've got you in there, Shere Khan. You're caught because of me, and there's no way I'm letting you out."

"Mowgli!" Shere Khan snarled.

But Mowgli was already running to the village, his heart thumping in time with his feet.

"Everyone! The tiger is trapped!" Mowgli called out joyfully. "Shere Khan has been trapped!"

The villagers rushed out of the elder's house. They lit torches, even though it was only early evening.

"What are you going on about, boy?" one of the men at the front of the crowd asked. "The tiger might hear you."

"There's no need to worry about the tiger." Mowgli panted. "The tiger is trapped! He can't do anything to anyone now."

Shamima pushed out from the crowd. "Mowgli! Mowgli, are you hurt?"

She cupped his face in her hands. Mowgli squirmed, trying to get away. "I'm fine. Really! But the tiger. I've trapped the tiger!"

The villagers looked doubtful, but Pavesh was

already shoving past them. "Come, let us see!"

"The wolf boy is probably telling a story," one man muttered. But they all walked toward the pit. Mowgli slipped out of Shamima's arms to trail behind.

When they reached the hole, Pavesh gazed down and gasped. Mowgli's face felt as if it would break in half from his big smile. He'd done something that even the grown-ups of the village couldn't do. They'd be impressed, right?

"Is this some kind of joke?" a village elder asked. "How could a boy like you take down the feared Shere Khan?"

Mowgli was speechless.

"Is this a trick by you and your wolf friends?" the same man asked. "If we try to drag the tiger out, he'll attack us, won't he?"

"It's not a trick," Mowgli protested.

"Azar, back down," Pavesh said.

"He's a wolf boy, after all. Who knows what he is up to?" the man shot back. Mowgli hung his head as they argued. The villagers were acting just like the wolf pack had after he'd chased off Shere Khan with the fire. The villagers still didn't trust him or accept him as one of them. He'd always be an outsider.

His hurt twisted into anger that jabbed between his shoulders like a stick. He walked away, while the villagers were still arguing. He'd show them! Quietly, quickly, he went to work. He dragged a large log toward the hole. He kicked one end into it.

"…and another thing…," the old man scolded Pavesh.

A low growl echoed eerily behind them, and they both fell silent. Shere Khan was climbing up the log, using it as a ramp! The villagers scattered, shrieking. Mowgli stayed still as the tiger prowled toward him.

What will Shere Khan do?

Shere Khan only gave him an evil glare before turning toward the jungle and disappearing into the trees. Mowgli watched him go. He hoped Shere Khan would leave him alone now. After all, Mowgli had been able to capture him, and the tigers wouldn't forget that. It was a law of the jungle to honor your enemy and accept when you'd lost, fair and square.

Mowgli returned to the village. As he approached, he heard the villagers talking about him. "Mowgli is a danger to us all. Shere Khan is on the loose."

"The chief of one of the largest villages offered us money if we caught Shere Khan and brought him his hide. Now we get nothing."

"The wolf boy makes me nervous," one woman said.

"Why does he have to be here with us?" said another.

Mowgli closed his eyes. *What should I do?* He tried to listen to his heart. And then it came to him.

"I'm not going to stay here," he told everyone. "I will leave the village so you can live in peace."

chapter 12

Leaving the village didn't feel the same as when he was forced out of the wolf pack with his eyes stinging and fingers a little burnt from the flame flower. Back then, he hadn't wanted to leave.

But now he was ready to move on.

His heart still ached a little as he looked

around the dazed crowd. If Shere Khan hadn't chased off his parents and left him to be raised by the wolves, would he be able to fit in here? Would they understand him better or, more important, would he be able to understand them and why they feared the jungle?

But he couldn't go back in time and change that now.

Pavesh stepped forward. "Mowgli," he said softly. "Where will you go?"

Mowgli looked over his shoulder. He sensed he was being watched. He let out a whistle. Baloo and Bagheera walked out of the trees, and Mowgli waved happily. Baloo waved back. Bagheera just licked one of his paws.

"These are my friends," Mowgli said proudly. "They're going to take me back where I belong. I belong in the jungle."

The woman from next door shook her head.

"How can a boy live by himself in the jungle with those animals?"

Mowgli knew he was too wild for the villagers, and they were too scared of everyone he loved. It was better to go now.

Shamima hugged him. "But the jungle just gave you back to me."

Mowgli hugged her back. For the first time, he realized that Shamima was smaller than he'd thought. No, he had grown. He was taller than when he first arrived at the village.

The thought made him proud.

Shamima had protected him and been strong for him when the villagers had tried to chase him off. A warm feeling spread through his chest. He leaned down to whisper in her ear. "I need to go. I'll be okay."

Shamima patted his cheek. "Yes, you will,

won't you? Take care of yourself and be strong, my little human-cub."

Mowgli nodded. Then he turned and walked back into the thick trees with Bagheera and Baloo at his side. Viaan and Sharaad ran up, panting.

"Is it over already?" Viaan asked.

"Yes." Bagheera nodded at Mowgli. "That was very brave, my little frog."

"Really?" Mowgli rubbed at his eyes. For some reason, they were stinging after saying goodbye, even though he did his best not to look back. "I'm glad. I wanted to be brave, even though it was scary at some parts."

"You did a good job," Baloo said reassuringly.

"Mother's going to be so proud when she hears," Viaan chimed in. "And Father, too."

"We really should stop calling you our little frog, though," Bagheera said thoughtfully. "A

frog couldn't capture Shere Khan. I liked what your human mother called you. Human-cub."

Mowgli turned the words over in his mind. Human-cub. Not a wolf. Not a man. But something in between.

He liked it, too.

It took him a moment to realize they had come to a sudden halt. Blinking, he looked up.

A beautiful wolf with a white-streaked coat and a large, teeth-baring smile stood in front of them. Behind her came another wolf, who stood strong and tall, with his tail wagging proudly.

"Mother. Father," Mowgli breathed.

"Mowgli, my little frog," Raksha said warmly. "My brave hero. You did it."

Mowgli swallowed a lump in his throat. "I missed you."

"Oh, Mowgli, I missed you, too. But we had

to send you away. We tried to protect you from Shere Khan."

"You did," Mowgli said fiercely. "You and Father both did. And I'm thankful for that. But I'm not a little frog now. I'm a human-cub."

She nodded gracefully. "Yes, you are. This is your jungle, Mowgli, the human-cub. And your pack, if you want to come back. Your father is still leader, and we'll make sure no one bothers you ever again."

Akeela licked his son's face. "Yes, Mowgli. You are our son, no matter what."

Mowgli looked around at his wolf parents, at his loyal brothers, at his teachers Bagheera and Baloo.

"This is my jungle," he said firmly. "And I will find my place in it, where I need to belong."

After all, he was not a wolf and not a man. He

was something very much in between, and there
was so much waiting for him to explore.

Mowgli the human-cub was home.

ghost
writer™

FUN

AND

PUZZLES

I never met Shere Khan (only Bagheera, who is super cool, too), but I think tigers are so strong, fierce, and beautiful. I ended up going into research mode to learn more about Bengal tigers—I couldn't help myself!

Tigers are among the largest of the big cats. A Bengal tiger can weigh between 240 and 500 pounds. That's equal to more than six of me!

The Bengal tiger is the national animal of India, and 70% of the world's tigers are found in India. Bengal tigers also live in Bangladesh, Nepal, and Bhutan. Unlike other cats, tigers love to swim!

Tigers have retractable claws, similar to house cats. This means they can pull them in when they're not needed.

A tiger's roar can be heard over two miles away!

Humans have cut down forests and hunted tigers for their hides. This has caused the Bengal tiger to become endangered—which means they could go out of existence forever if they're not properly cared for. A hundred years ago, there were over 100,000 tigers. Today, only about 2,500 Bengal tigers live in the wild.

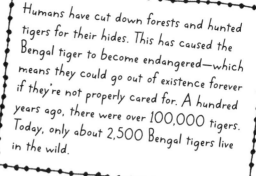

A tiger has its own camou-flage: stripes! They let the tiger blend into the jungle while it's hunting. No two tigers have the same stripe pattern, just like no two humans have the same fingerprints. And if you shave off a tiger's fur, you'll see the exact same stripes on its skin. So unique!

Tigers are carnivores, or meat eaters. They sneak up on their prey and—BAM!—surprise attack. They hunt in the early morning or late evening and sleep in the shade during the day.

The Bengal tiger's teeth are about 3 inches long! That's as long as an adult's index finger.

Curtis's Jungle Jokes

Mowgli's story didn't exactly have me rolling around laughing. Being kicked out of the wolf pack, escaping the monkeys, and battling a mean tiger are way serious. But, hey, he handled it like a pro, and who says the jungle can't be funny? Here are some animal jokes that always make me and my friends crack up.

What did the leopard say after finishing his meal?
That really hit the spot!

Where do hippopotamuses keep their money?
In the riverbank.

What's as big as an elephant but weighs nothing?
An elephant's shadow.

What do monkeys sing at Christmas?
"Jungle Bells."

What's the best thing about deadly snakes?

They've got poison-ality.

Which snakes are found on cars?

Windshield vipers.

How do you know when there's an elephant under your bed?

When your nose touches the ceiling.

What do you call bears with no ears?

B!

What do you call a lost wolf?

A where-wolf!

What did one wolf say to the other?

"Howl's it going?"

On which side does a tiger have the most stripes?

On the outside.

Chevon's Brain-Bender Quiz

Bagheera and Baloo know how to talk to all the animals. (That's how they find the best fruit!) They pay attention—which I understand, since I try not to miss the details when I read a book. What about you? Take my brain-bender quiz to see how closely you read this story.

1. A group of wolves is called a _____.

    a. flock

    b. herd

    c. pack

    d. gaggle

2. Wolves live in a _____.

    a. den

    b. kitchen

    c. nest

    d. tent

3. What do the animals call fire?

> a. hot stuff
>
> b. flame flower
>
> c. dancing ember
>
> d. flame thrower

4. Where do the monkeys take Mowgli?

> a. The hidden Hut of the Monkey Master
>
> b. The hidden Fortress of the Monkey Clan
>
> c. The hidden City of the Monkey King
>
> d. The hidden Tree House of the Monkey Prince

5. Cows like to talk about _____.

> a. their favorite flavor of ice cream
>
> b. baseball
>
> c. cowbells
>
> d. the weather

6. Shere Khan didn't see the hole Mowgli had dug, because it was covered with _____.

> a. a net
>
> b. a blanket
>
> c. large leaves
>
> d. logs

Check your answers on page 137.

Ruben's Scramble

The jungle is home to all kinds of creatures. Can you unscramble the letters to find the names of these animals?

THY**P**ON _____

KOYME**N** _____

CERNOO**S**HRI _____

THOSL **A**REB _____

PHELNE**T**A _____

CLODIC**R**OE _____

KC**E**GO _____

Now write down all the bolded letters and unscramble them to decode the mystery animal: _____

Answers on page 137.

The Curtis Challenge

Mowgli grew up in the wolf pack, and he called them his family. Sometimes you have more than one wolf pack. I'm really lucky, because not only do I have my parents, my sister, Donna, and our dog, Rocco, but I also have my basketball buds and our bookstore crew—thanks to Ghostwriter. Think about who you're thankful for in your own wolf pack before taking my challenge out for a spin!

Can you take the letters in the words **WOLF PACK** and make smaller words? How many can you make?

Here are a few words to get you started:

cow   cloak   foal

Here's how to keep score

Each 3-letter word = 1 point

Each 4-letter word = 2 points

Each 5-letter word = 3 points

Each word with 6 letters or more = 4 points

Chevon's Amazing Definition Game

I'd love to learn how to talk to animals, like Mowgli can. I wonder what happens when animals don't understand something other animals say. Do you think they have animal dictionaries?

Draw a line connecting the vocabulary word from the story with the correct definition.

1. Scuffle

a. a glowing piece of coal or wood in the ashes from a fire

2. Pierce

b. careful about staying away from danger

3. Ember

c. a long piece of material draped around the body like a dress, worn by women in Southeast Asia

4. Snarl

d. to make a hole in or through

5. Cautious

e. seeds of a type of plant called a legume. Other legumes are chickpeas and peanuts

6. Sari

f. an angry growl, or to say with a growl

7. Lentils

g. a fight in a rough, confused way

Answers on page 137.

Ruben's (and Grandpa's) Reading List

When you own a bookstore, you're probably a total book expert, like my grandpa. We made this reading list together. (Okay, maybe he did most of it, but I helped.)

If you liked *The Jungle Book*, here are some other books we think you'll enjoy.

Books with Talking Animals

The One and Only Ivan by Katherine Applegate

Charlotte's Web by E. B. White

Fantastic Mr. Fox by Roald Dahl

The Wild Robot by Peter Brown

Books that Take Place in India

The Night Diary by Veera Hiranandani

The Bridge Home by Padma Venkatraman

A Graphic Novel with Talking Animals *and* India!

Pashmina by Nidhi Chanani

Donna Gets Crafty:
Accordion Paper Snakes

I love to make accordion paper snakes. I've decorated my room with them—and they're fun to play with, too! I can't wait until my brother, Curtis, comes home from school. I'm making a snake that wraps *all the way around* our bedroom. He's going to be SO SURPRISED.

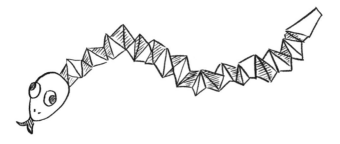

What you need:

- construction paper in two colors
- tape
- glue
- black marker
- googly eyes (if you have them)
- red construction paper

1. With the help of an adult, cut three or four strips from the paper. The strips should all be about the same width and length. The easiest way to do this is to fold a piece of paper in half, then fold it in half again and again and again. Unfold the paper and use your scissors to cut along the fold lines. Do this for each paper color.

2. Take a strip of each paper color. Place them in an L shape. Tape them together where they overlap.

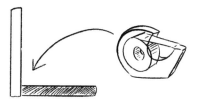

3. Now it's time to start folding the strips into an accordion. Fold the horizontal strip over the vertical strip. Crease the fold to make another L shape.

4. Now fold the strips in the other direction. Keep repeating.

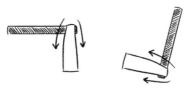

5. Before you run out of paper, cut off one of the strips of paper. Tape the end of the short strip to the longer strip so your snake doesn't unravel. Leave the end of the longer paper strip unfolded.

6. Cut a snake-shaped head out of a piece of construction paper. You can glue on googly eyes or draw eyes and nostrils with a black marker. Cut a tongue from red construction paper and glue it onto the snake's head. Tape the head onto the end of the long paper strip.

7. Do you want to make a longer snake? Just attach several strips of the same color together with glue or tape. (When I need a break from folding, I put tape on where I've ended and then remove it when I'm ready to start again.)

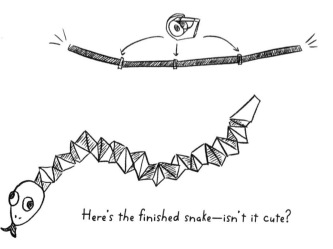

Here's the finished snake—isn't it cute?

Ghostwriter's Secret Message

Ghostwriter has a question for you. Use the clues below to decode the secret answer.

Spinoza is a talkative alley cat with a lot of attitude. When Ruben's grandma was alive, Spinoza visited whenever she was hungry (and for a scratch behind her ears). Where did Spinoza go to get fed?

First two letters of second-oldest wolf brother's name ___ ___

Fifth letter of the main character's name ___

Last two letters of the wolf father's name ___ ___

Fourth letter of the main character's name ___

Third letter of the tiger's name ___

First letter of the panther's name ___

Last two letters of the bear's name ___ ___

First letter of the snake's name ___

First letter of the tiger's name ___

Answer: ___ ___ ___ ___ ___ ___   ___ ___ ___ ___ ___

Answers

Chevon's Brain-Bender Quiz: 1. c, 2. a, 3. b, 4. c, 5. d, 6. c

Ruben's Scramble: python, monkey, rhinoceros, sloth bear, elephant, crocodile, gecko

Mystery animal: panther

Chevon's Amazing Definition Game: 1. g, 2. d, 3. a, 4. f, 5. b, 6. c, 7. e

Ghostwriter's Secret Message: VILLAGE BOOKS

About the Authors

Rudyard Kipling was born in 1865 in Bombay (now Mumbai), India. When he was six years old, he and his sister were sent to England for school. He returned to India as a young adult and worked as a journalist. He married an American woman and moved to the United States. While living in Vermont, he wrote *The Jungle Book* for his baby daughter. He returned to England and, in 1907, was the first English writer to be awarded the Nobel Prize in Literature. He died in 1936.

 Karuna Riazi is a born-and-raised New Yorker, with a loving, large extended family and the rather trying experience of being the eldest sibling in her particular clan. She is an online diversity advocate, blogger, and educator, and the author of *The Gauntlet* and *The Battle*, both from Simon and Schuster's *Salaam Reads* imprint. Karuna is fond of tea, Korean dramas, writing about tough girls forging their own paths toward their destinies, and baking new delectable treats for friends and family to relish.